CW00857975

Handersen Publishing, LLC
Lincoln, Nebraska

Clarissa

This book is a work of fiction. All characters and other incidents are a product of the author's imagination, and locales are used in a fictitious manner. Any resemblance to actual events, or persons, living or dead, is entirely coincidental.

Library of Congress Cataloging-in-Publication Data

Names: Spudich, Giulietta M, author. Title: Clarissa / Giulietta M Spudich. Description: Lincoln, Nebraska : Handersen Publishing, LLC, [2020] | Audience: Ages 7-10. | Audience: Grades 2-3. | Summary: "After her mother's death, Clarissa doesn't know how to connect with her distant father. Her only friend is an oak tree with whom she can tell her deepest secrets. When she discovers a mysterious key that unleashes a long-forgotten fire spirit, she must find her voice to protect those she loves"-- Provided by publisher. Identifiers: LCCN 2020034800 (print) | LCCN 2020034801 (ebook) | ISBN 9781647030360 (paperback) | ISBN 9781647030377 (hardback) | ISBN 9781647030384 (mobi) Classification: LCC PZ7.1.S71784 Cl 2020 (print) | LCC PZ7.1.S71784 (ebook) | DDC [Fic]--dc23
LC record available at https://lccn.loc.gov/2020034800
LC ebook record available at https://lccn.loc.gov/2020034801

Author Website: www.ElementGirls.org
Publisher Website: www.handersenpublishing.com
Publisher Email: editors@handersenpublishing.com

Clarissa

Giulietta M. Spudich

Handersen Publishing, LLC
Lincoln, Nebraska

Come into my sheltering arms,
my branches tall, my branches strong.
I'll hold you while the moon goes down
and listen to your secrets.

Squirrel and bird and little girl,
in my home of wood come curl.
I'll tell you of the olden days
from my heartwood deepest.

Love,
Oak

Chapter One

$\mathscr{A}$ cozy house with a large garden stood in the great, flat part of England known as the fens. Though the house was gray where it used to be white, and the windows had been patched many times to keep out the weather, it was comfortable and dry inside. It was home to the Gentle family, and had belonged to them for generations.

The Gentles spent evenings by the fire in the living room full of soft places to sit. Mr. Gentle stayed for hours on the armchair with his laptop computer. Edmund, who was almost three but didn't talk yet, stretched out on the sofa. Clarissa preferred the pillows on the floor and was often joined by Shadow.

Shadow was eleven just like Clarissa. In human years, eleven was pretty young. In cat years it was old, so he just curled up on the pillows or her lap and slept.

Tonight, though, Clarissa was not in the house. She was feeling the chill in the darkening night from her favorite place to sit–the oak tree in their big garden. It was cloudy, and the half-moon was almost hidden.

The tree had branches evenly spaced from low to high and it liked when Clarissa sat in them. She knew because it told her. Her father couldn't hear it talk, but he was an adult and adults miss many things. Her little brother Edmund wouldn't tell her if he could hear it or not. So, she might be the only one.

Her favorite tales Oak told were about the marsh sprites and will-o'-the-wisps. The tree remembered them from the old days. Long ago, the wisps would guide lost travelers to safety in the night, or to their doom. It depended on the wisp.

Tonight, though, she wasn't in the mood for a story. She was feeling lonely and just wanted to rest on a branch. Her long ponytail was getting caught in the grooves in the bark. A knot of wood poked her thigh. She shifted position on the usually comfortable branch. She couldn't even sit right.

A sob escaped her.

"Tell me child," Oak said in a voice like the wind through tall grass. "Why are you so sad?"

A tear slid down Clarissa's cheek and she wiped it away angrily. Her day had been a bad day, an awful day. At school, she misspelled 'lightning', and because it was the third time that week, the teacher Mrs. Wilkes moved her name down a rung on the spelling ladder. Then Mrs. Wilkes asked her what was wrong and why she wasn't doing as well at school as normal.

Nothing was wrong, and she wanted to tell Mrs. Wilkes she was doing very well at school, thank you. She knew three answers to questions asked in class that day. She didn't wave her hand around or shout out, but she did know the answers.

Preeti, her best and only friend, said Clarissa

should be louder and say what she knew. But Clarissa just couldn't speak up. Her voice wouldn't come even when she wanted it to.

To make it all worse, dinner was mashed potatoes, mushy peas and soggy nut roast. It was all too squishy to enjoy. That made her miss Mum's food. Thinking about it made her miss Mum with an awful pain in her heart.

When Mum was alive she cooked every night. Dad had gotten better at cooking over the last three years, but his food was still hard to eat.

If things weren't bad enough, just after dinner, Edmund broke her wooden dragonfly. Dad only told her that all toys break. She knew if Edmund's toy broke, Dad would be nice to him and give him extra dessert. But she was only told to be a big girl. That's when she came outside in the moonlight to find company in the oak tree.

She didn't tell the tree any of that. It all felt too much to say. So, she said nothing, but gave the branch she was sitting on a big hug. She pressed her wet face against its rough bark. It felt good to hold a strong, friendly branch.

"It's been a long, dry summer," the tree said.

"Yes, I know," Clarissa replied. "Normally it rains a lot. My dad said the weather was weird this year."

"You gave me water when I asked," the tree said. "My bark stayed thick and my leaves stayed green."

"I'm glad you aren't all dried up and brown," she said. Her neighbor's birch tree barely had any leaves left.

"I would like to help you, as you helped me," the tree said. A leaf tickled Clarissa's cheek, but she didn't laugh.

"How?" she asked.

"I will give you a gift," the tree said.

Her tears stopped. A gift could at least make up for the broken dragonfly. She wondered what it was.

Maybe it was a crown of leaves like the one the tree gave her on her tenth birthday last year. Or it could be a bird's nest the tree caught in its twisted branches, empty of eggs, of course.

"Look in my roots," the tree said. "Dig on the north side."

Clarissa lowered herself down to the branch beneath and jumped to the ground. She smoothed the dirt away on the tree's north side. She knew it was north because her dad had shown her where the North Star was one night and she never forgot.

She dug with a stone. A dull, metal shine caught the moonlight. She rubbed the dirt away. The object was small, and fit in her hand.

It was a key.

Chapter Two

Clouds moved fast in the night sky. The moon shone soft light on the oak tree and Clarissa. She held the key up to see it better.

It was an old key, with a long body and fancy top. She pressed it to her nose. It smelled like metal.

"What does it open?" she asked.

"That I do not know," the tree said. "Except I have never known a key like it."

"Maybe it opens a door," she said.

"All keys unlock something," Oak said. "Perhaps this key is to a door leading to new places. A door opened lets new things that were blocked come to us."

"Where did you find this key?" Clarissa asked.

"I found it deep in the ground one summer when my roots grew down, searching for water," the tree said. "One hundred years ago."

"You kept it all this time?" Clarissa asked.

"I kept it deep down," the tree said. "Willow thought it was a good idea to give it to you."

A willow tree stood at the edge of their garden, which seemed too far away for a conversation. Plus the only tree that ever spoke to Clarissa was the oak. She suddenly had too many questions, and they all tumbled out of her at once.

"How do you talk to the willow tree?" Clarissa asked. "Why doesn't it talk to me? Why does Willow want to give me the key?"

The tree laughed, a booming sound that shook its branches.

"You have too many questions," the tree said. "I will answer one."

Clarissa thought hard. Which was the best question to pick?

"Why does Willow want to give me the key?" she asked.

"Willow told me that a fire is coming," the tree said. "It will start with a girl and a key."

"Fire?" Clarissa said. "How can a fire come from a key?"

"Perhaps the key opens a door to fire," Oak said, rustling its branches. "Fire has the ability to transform things, to change them. How exciting, even for an old tree like me who has seen so many things."

"Why are you happy about it?" Clarissa asked. "Isn't fire dangerous for trees?"

The tree sighed and its leaves shook.

"Fire uncontrolled is dangerous," the tree said. "But fire has been gone from our land for a long time."

She tried to ask the oak tree more questions.

"It is time for me to watch the moon and stars, and be quiet," Oak said. It stopped rustling and stood still.

The oak got tired of talking more often these days.

She wished she could get an answer to her questions. But she wanted to be a good friend and let Oak rest. She wrapped her arms around the trunk, kissed a knot, and said thank you.

She held the key tight in her hand.

She waved to Willow and shouted a thank you, wondering if it could really hear her. Oak could, so why not Willow?

She took one long, deep breath of the damp night air. One of her favorite smells was the river, which was only a short walk away. She could smell it now—rich and damp with a green scent of plants.

After a good sniff, she went into the house. She yelled a "good night" to Dad who was still on his laptop in the living room. He grunted in reply.

Her bedroom was upstairs. After brushing the knots out of her long, light-brown hair, she knelt at her bed to send love to her mum like every night.

Three years ago, when Mum died and Edmund was born, the tree started to speak and give her gifts. Dad never believed her about the talking oak tree, but she knew Mum would.

Clarissa pulled out her special journal, the one with jasmine flowers on the cover. It wasn't a journal for recording her day or writing stories. It was more special than that.

She wrote to Mum in it.

Dear Mum,

I had a bad day at school. My teacher thought I didn't know the answers, but I did. My friend Preeti thinks I should speak up in class, but it's hard. Oh well.

Edmund broke my wooden dragonfly. I'm not mad, just sad. He can't help it, he's only two-almost-three.

But none of that matters. Oak gave me a gift! It's an old key. I'm sure it is magic.

Oak said it might open the door to a fire. That sounds sort of scary and sort of exciting too.

I can't wait to go exploring and find the door it opens.

Love you 'til the end of time,
Clarissa

She climbed under the covers. Clarissa wasn't sad about her day anymore, or even about Mum. She was excited to explore her new gift. She fell asleep quickly, her hand curled around the key.

Chapter Three

*O*n Saturday she woke up early. Streaks of morning sun shone through her window. She was ready to search for a secret door.

Clarissa slipped the fancy key in her pocket and hopped down the stairs. But as she wolfed down a bowl of cereal, Dad came in looking tired.

"We need to go to the museum," he said, pulling his short, graying hair. "I've got some work to do."

Clarissa dropped her spoon with a plop. The only cool thing at the museum was the basement, where she wasn't allowed. Ancient bones, old spears and shields, even a mummy were stored in the basement collection. She would love to see all of it.

But Clarissa and Edmund were only allowed in the public part of the museum, where just some of the artifacts were. The same old artifacts she had seen a million times.

At the museum, Dad asked one of the volunteers to keep an eye on Clarissa and Edmund while he went to his office. Edmund immediately ran to the children's cart. He grabbed a drawing of a knight to color in and a red crayon. She took his hand and they walked to the Viking section.

They sat in front of a familiar spear and shield in the Viking section. The volunteer left them and Edmund smiled a gap-toothed smile at her. She responded with a thumbs-up. She knew it was her brother's favorite section too.

Clarissa took out her sketchpad and charcoal. It wasn't the first time she'd tried to draw the shield, but she had never used charcoal before. So, at least it would be kind of new.

Halfway through drawing, Clarissa heard a familiar voice. It was the loud, gushing voice of Dr.

Vidal, one of Dad's professor friends who worked in the museum.

Dr. Vidal's dark, glossy hair flowed around her shoulders, and she had on a silk, flowery blouse. Her face was lit up as she talked to a tall man with a dark-brown ponytail.

"These potion bottles were found in East Anglia, at a site close-by," Dr. Vidal explained to the man. Small, glass potion bottles sat next to the wooden wands in the medieval section.

"Look, a love potion," Dr. Vidal said. A bottle shaped like a heart stood among the others on the shelf.

"It matches the charm you gave me!" Dr. Vidal said, her cheeks red. She lifted her bracelet up. It made a jangly sound when she shook it.

"Oh yeah," the man said with a toothy smile. "Never mind the love potion—they are common. What's this one with the flame on it?" he asked, reaching toward a red bottle. His voice was smooth and as loud as Dr. Vidal's.

"That one is new," Dr. Vidal said. "A woman

donated it recently–her grandmother made potions. We're not sure what it does."

"There is actually liquid inside," he said and took the stopper out of the bottle. Clarissa gasped. Not only were you never supposed to touch anything in the museum, you certainly weren't allowed to open anything. She tried to call out to him. Her voice wouldn't come, though.

"You aren't supposed to open the bottles, love," Dr. Vidal said, batting her eyes and taking the bottle away from the man. She replaced the stopper and put the bottle back on the shelf.

"It smells like a fire caller, a potion to call in a fire spirit," he said. "Those are incredibly rare, even in medieval times."

"You know so much!" Dr. Vidal said, leaning on his arm. "The medieval age is not my focus."

"We still have potions in our time, too," the man said and hugged Dr. Vidal with one long arm. "People like the grandmother who made the fire caller are still crafting them."

"Well, give me the Vikings any day," Dr. Vidal said. "We have the best display here."

At that point she turned to the section Clarissa was sitting in.

"Darling Clarissa!" Dr. Vidal said and beamed at her. "And your sweet brother Edmund." Dr. Vidal rushed over and gave Clarissa a too-tight hug.

"How are you?" Dr. Vidal said, her big brown eyes extra large.

Before Clarissa could answer, Dr. Vidal turned to the man with the ponytail.

"Poor darlings, they lost their mum what was it— two years ago?" Dr. Vidal blinked at Clarissa with big eyes, clearly expecting an answer.

"Three years in December," Clarissa said. Her throat felt tight and her voice came out small.

"Of course, sweet Edmund's birthday," she said, looking extra sad.

Clarissa didn't like how Dr. Vidal was looking at her. She wasn't feeling sad today. In fact she was feeling happy about how her charcoal shield was turning out. Better than when she did it in colored pens.

Edmund crept closer to Clarissa and climbed in her lap. He hung on tight to his red crayon.

"You're such a good sister, looking after him," Dr. Vidal said. "Where's your dad? Let me guess, in his office?"

Clarissa nodded.

"Well, hope you two are having fun," Dr. Vidal said. "I was just telling Kurt that my favorite display is the Viking section. You're just like me."

Clarissa wasn't just like Dr. Vidal. She was just like Mum, who loved the Viking section best. But she didn't say anything.

The man with the long ponytail leaned towards Clarissa.

"We've been in the potions," Kurt said and winked. He was tall, and Clarissa felt her hands go clammy. She wasn't used to speaking to adults she didn't know.

Edmund wrapped his arms around Clarissa's middle, and peeped out from under her arm with big eyes.

"All right children, we'll let you get on with your drawings," Dr. Vidal said. "Goodbye, my darlings." She blew kisses to them as she and Kurt left the section.

Edmund stuck his paper in front of Clarissa's face as soon as they left. She studied the red crayon marks across the knight. He never stayed in the lines when he colored.

"Great, Edmund," Clarissa said. "Mum would have liked it. This was her favorite section too, just like us."

Edmund grinned at her.

"I have something to show you," Clarissa said. Edmund looked at her sketchpad, but Clarissa pulled the old metal key out of her pocket.

"It's very old," Clarissa said.

Edmund wrapped his chubby hand around the key. His eyebrows rose.

"I don't know what it opens either," Clarissa said. "But I bet it's an old door to something really amazing." She tickled him and he giggled.

Edmund drew the key to his mouth. Clarissa took it back from him before he ate it.

She took it as a good sign. When Edmund tried to eat something, it met with his approval.

Chapter Four

*D*ad still wasn't back, so Clarissa drew a sword and shield on the back of Edmund's paper for him to color in. Tired of sketching, she put down her charcoal pencil.

The display hadn't changed since the last time she saw it. The wooden boat at the back had been there as long as Clarissa could remember. Mum even drew it one time and let Clarissa color it in. She remembered using a blue and a purple crayon, and staying in the lines.

Edmund had been there too, as a bump in Mum's belly. That's when Mum had to rest a lot, especially since her bump was big. She leaned against Dad as they stood watching Clarissa color. He rubbed her shoulders and made her laugh. That was back when Dad made jokes.

Her mum's hair was long and light, just like Clarissa's. Dad's hair was a solid brown. Mum used to joke that Dad's hair must be made of chocolate since it was the same color as Clarissa's favorite ice cream.

Edmund broke her out of remembering by standing up. He was looking at something behind them. Dad came over. He wasn't laughing or joking. His gray hair stuck up a little and he had a small frown.

"I'm all done for now," Dad said. "Ice cream?"

Even though Mum wasn't around and Dad didn't joke, at least there was still ice cream.

At the ice cream parlor, Clarissa saw a familiar face.

"Preeti!" Clarissa grinned at her school friend and waved. Preeti waved back. She had on a cheerful, pink top. Her curly hair was tied back in a ponytail, just like Clarissa's.

Preeti was with three boys, all younger than her, and her mum. They got cones and came over to the table.

Preeti scooted next to Clarissa and touched ice creams. Clarissa's made a chocolate kiss mark on Preeti's lemon swirl.

Edmund stared at Preeti's ice cream cone and tried to wobble his own chocolate cone towards hers. Clarissa quickly righted his hand before the ice cream could fall.

"You can try that when you're older, Ed," Clarissa said. He held his cone with both hands and licked big.

Preeti's mum swooped over to the table. She had on a beautiful purple and gold Indian tunic and Clarissa was momentarily caught up in its pattern.

"Hello, Mr. Gentle," Preeti's mum said to Dad, who was eating his mint chocolate chip with a spoon.

"Hello Mrs..." Dad said.

"I'm Uma Patel, Preeti's mum," she said. "Call me Uma."

"Tom," Dad said, nodding at her.

"I recognize you from the parent's meeting at the school," she said.

"Ah yes," Dad said and blinked. Clarissa could tell he didn't remember.

"May we?" she asked and pulled up a chair. Dad nodded and soon they were all sitting together. The two older boys tried to lick each other's ice creams. The smallest boy looked about Edmund's age. He and Edmund stared at each other.

"So, what's new?" Preeti leaned over to Clarissa.

Clarissa thought. What could she tell her friend? The Viking morning wasn't all that interesting.

She pulled out the key.

"Look what I found!" Clarissa said. "Actually, a tree gave it to me."

Preeti laughed a loud and happy laugh.

"Oh, C, you're so funny!" she said. "A tree!" she snorted.

"Anyway, what do you think it opens?" Clarissa asked.

Preeti held it up to the light.

"A secret garden?" she said. They had just been reading The Secret Garden in school.

"Maybe," Clarissa said. "If there's time later, I'm going to go looking for a locked gate."

"One covered in ivy," Preeti said. "I'll look too! If I find, anything I'll tell you on Monday."

"Chocolate on the nose!" the boy Edmund's age screamed across the table to Edmund.

Clarissa took a tissue and cleaned Edmund's nose. It was pointless, though. He had a whole cone of ice cream to eat, and by the end, it would be all over his face.

"That's Nimesh," Preeti said and rolled her eyes. "He's very clean."

Clarissa looked at Nimesh with amazement. Even though he was eating an ice cream cone, none of it showed on his face.

"Name?" the boy shouted to Edmund. "Name!"

"He's Edmund," Clarissa said. "He doesn't talk yet."

"What's wrong with him?" an older boy said. "Why doesn't he talk?"

"Hush, Jay, " Preeti's mum said to the boy. "Some children take longer to speak than others."

Preeti's mum looked at Dad with big eyes.

"I'm sure he'll start speaking up a storm soon," she said. "And Clarissa looks like she is doing so well. Last time I saw her she was all in black. And now…"

Preeti's mum turned to Clarissa.

"Look at your lovely blue top," she said. Clarissa felt a blush creep to her cheeks. She was embarrassed about her black-clothes period. For a year after Mum died, she only wore black and hardly spoke. She would like to forget about it, but her classmates still called her "Clarissa the Crow."

Only Preeti had dared to sit next to her at lunch that year. And Preeti had never called her that name at all.

"We need to get moving," Dad said, easing up from the table. "Very nice to meet you…Uma."

"We must get together sometime with our families," Preeti's mum said. "Come for dinner sometime."

Dad nodded. They left the ice cream shop and headed to the car.

"Good that you have a friend," Dad said to Clarissa.

"Yeah, Preeti's nice," Clarissa said. "Can we go to her house for dinner sometime?"

"When, is the question," Dad said. "I'm just so busy."

Clarissa frowned. She was tired of eating Dad's cooking or the same old pizza takeaway.

She could still taste the ice cream on her lips. At least that was always good.

She clutched the key in her pocket. Was Preeti right? Did it open a gate to a secret garden?

"Have you got homework to do?" Dad asked.

"Yeah," Clarissa said, her heart sinking.

"Once we get home, let's have homework hour," Dad said.

Clarissa nodded.

It seemed like Dad only paid attention to what she was doing when she had homework.

The search for the secret door would have to wait.

Chapter Five

Sunday rained and rained. Then it was school all week. So, it wasn't until Saturday came around again that Clarissa could search for the secret door.

She woke up early to a cloudy day. She slipped the fancy key in her pocket and hopped down the stairs. But as she guzzled a glass of orange juice, Dad came in looking tired.

"We need to go to the museum," he said.

"Again?" Clarissa asked. Her mood darkened.

"Yes," Dad said. "Dr. Vidal just called me. One of the bottles of potion from the medieval period is missing."

Clarissa rested her head on the table. She wanted to search for the secret door. The museum wasn't even open yet. Edmund and Clarissa were looking at a long, boring morning in Dad's dusty office.

"We'll pick up some breakfast burritos," Dad said.

That only made things a little better.

Shadow met her eye and meowed sadly. Clarissa guessed he knew he'd be alone all day with his humans gone to Dad's museum office.

Dad dropped them in his dusty office with dirty windows, and left them in there to eat the burritos. Clarissa pulled a Templar Knight coloring book out of her bag for Edmund. Once he was coloring at Dad's desk, she surfed the Internet for old keys on Dad's computer. She didn't find any pictures of ones that looked like hers, though.

It was a whole hour before Dad came back. Dr. Vidal was with him. Her long, black hair was loose and flowing. With red lipstick on, she looked ready for a party. But her eyebrows were pinched and she frowned.

Clarissa winced as she waited for Dr. Vidal to swoop in and hug her too tight. But Dr. Vidal didn't even seem to see Clarissa and Edmund. She was talking to Dad.

Dad grabbed a big binder off his shelf while Dr. Vidal spoke in quick and panicked tones. Dad's hair was all sticking up. He put the binder down with a thud. A cloud of dust floated over Edmund's coloring book.

Her little brother frowned. He took his book away to a corner and sat there.

"No one has used their key card to get in since yesterday at 7 pm," Dr. Vidal said, her dark eyes large.

"Were the doors and windows closed and locked when you got here?" Dad asked.

"Yes. There were no signs of a break-in," she said. "The alarm wasn't set, but you know how Sophie forgets…"

Clarissa thought only her dad and Dr. Vidal worked with the museum collection, so she asked, "Who's Sophie?"

"Our volunteer," Dr. Vidal said and blinked at Clarissa. "Oh hello, my dear, how are you?" She grabbed Clarissa and kissed her.

Thick rose-scented perfume filled Clarissa's nose. She sneezed.

"Is this the missing bottle, Mandy?" Dad asked. He held up the binder to show a photo of a small, red bottle with a cork in it. It was made of glass and had a flame painted on it in black.

"That one, yes," Dr. Vidal said, leaning over his shoulder. "All the other medieval objects were in their places."

Clarissa recognized the bottle. The man with Dr. Vidal had been interested in it last weekend at the museum. She remembered that his name began with a k…what was it?

"These potion bottles really should be in a glass case," her dad said, reading the text under the picture.

Dr. Vidal rolled her eyes.

"Absolutely," she said. "But they aren't."

"I'm…worried," Dr. Vidal said and pinched the

bridge of her nose. "She's a sweet girl, but perhaps she took it for curiosity?"

"You think Sophie took it?" Dad said. "Why don't we ring her and ask?"

Dr. Vidal took her phone out. She held the phone to her ear. Then she sighed deeply and hung up.

"Sophie isn't home," Dr. Vidal said, rolling her eyes. "I'll keep trying to reach her. Though I need to go home and pack for Greece."

"Greece?" Dad asked. "Oh yes, your holiday with…Kurt, is it?"

Dr. Vidal nodded, smiling.

Clarissa swallowed hard. She didn't like speaking up, but she was too curious not to.

"Is that the man I saw you with at the museum?" Clarissa asked. Her voice came out quiet, but at least it came out.

"Yes, he's my boyfriend," she said. "Kurt is so wonderful, so smart. He knows all about potions. They can be very powerful."

"Powerful?" Clarissa asked. She studied the charm on Dr. Vidal's silver bracelet. It was shaped like a love potion—a bottle in the shape of a heart.

36

"Potions can be used to cast spells," Dr. Vidal said, looking dreamy.

"What kind of spells?" Clarissa asked. But Dad took her arm.

"People believed in magic potions a long time ago," Dad said. "But, of course today we know there is no such thing as magic." He peered directly into her eyes.

As his light-brown eyes stared into hers, Clarissa realized there were spots of green in them. She couldn't remember the last time he had really looked at her.

"Right, Clarissa?" Dad said. "Magic isn't real."

Clarissa blinked. Of course magic was real. Her best friend was a talking tree. She didn't say anything, though. She knew Dad wouldn't like to hear it.

So, she just shrugged.

"Meanwhile, we have more important things to do," Dad said to Dr. Vidal. "I'm going to check the visitor book."

He left the office.

Dr. Vidal studied Clarissa with one eyebrow raised.

"You believe in magic, don't you?" Dr. Vidal said.

Clarissa nodded. She almost told the professor about the talking tree. But she wasn't sure she trusted Dr. Vidal and her too-tight hugs.

"Kurt told me some potions can be used to summon spirits," Dr. Vidal said in a loud whisper.

"You mean ghosts?" Clarissa asked.

"He was talking about elemental spirits," Dr. Vidal said. "Wind, fire—that sort of thing. Kurt said they are good protection against enemies."

"I don't have any enemies," Clarissa said.

"Kurt has enemies who want his money," Dr. Vidal said, biting her lip. "I'm worried about him."

"Does your boyfriend have a lot of money?" Clarissa asked.

"Oh no," Dr. Vidal said. "But he bets on horse racing and I guess he might owe some money."

"Isn't that gambling?" Clarissa asked.

Dr. Vidal laughed, though it sounded more like a shriek.

"Kurt's just having fun," Dr. Vidal said. "There's nothing wrong with it. He is just in a little trouble."

"Wait–did Kurt take the potion?" Clarissa asked. "To protect himself from his enemies?"

"What?" Dr. Vidal said and dropped her phone. Edmund watched it bounce on the floor and separate from its case.

"Kurt would never do anything wrong," Dr. Vidal said as she picked the phone up and put it back together.

Her charm bracelet jingled.

"Kurt is wonderful," Dr. Vidal said, swooning with one hand on her heart. "If Kurt took the potion it is because it was the right thing to do."

Clarissa felt her face grow hot.

The Dr. Vidal she knew would never be OK with someone stealing an artifact from the museum.

Clarissa examined the charm on the jangling bracelet peeping out from Dr. Vidal's floral sleeve.

The charm was shaped like a love potion.

Could Dr. Vidal be under Kurt's spell?

Chapter Six

$\mathcal{D}$ad walked in with a frown.

"There is no one in the visitor book except Kurt," Dad said.

"Oh yes," Dr. Vidal said and shriek-laughed again. "He helped me with some things yesterday, so I would be ready for our holiday."

"You may need to delay going to Greece," Dad said. This caused Dr. Vidal to frown darkly as well.

"We can't. Why would we delay it?" she asked.

"Well, we may need to phone the police," her dad said, causing even Edmund to raise his head and pay attention. "We have many old and priceless items. If someone can break in once, they can do it again."

"But what if Sophie has put it somewhere?" Dr. Vidal said. "How about I try to reach her in an hour or two. If I can't speak with her by the evening, we'll phone the police then."

"I am not sure about waiting that long," her dad said.

"We risk being in a news story if we call the police," she said. "If it seems we have bad security, the University may close our little museum."

Clarissa thought it was a good idea to call the police. Maybe they would find the red bottle and they could all go home.

Then she could finally search for the secret door that her key unlocked.

Her dad pulled at his hair again.

"All right, I suppose we can wait until we talk to Sophie," he said. "I'll go down and check the basement collection. Maybe the bottle was damaged and she put it there for safe-keeping."

"I looked for the potion there myself," Dr. Vidal said. "Double check, though, by all means."

Dad put his glasses down and massaged his forehead.

Clarissa wanted to tell Dad what Dr. Vidal said about Kurt having enemies. Maybe Kurt took the potion. He had a motive, and Clarissa learned at school that a motive was a reason someone did something. Like take something that didn't belong to him.

Plus, the basement collection was something Clarissa had always wanted to see. Maybe she could even sketch something down there. Dad would talk about the artifacts sometimes. Once Dad said there was a mummy in a glass case.

Mum used to say he had bone dust in his hair when he got home. So, she knew there were bones in the basement.

Clarissa grabbed her bag with her sketchpad in it and followed her dad into the hallway.

"Take me to the basement," Clarissa said. "I need to tell you something."

"Stay here and watch your brother," he said.

"Please?" she asked. "Edmund's just coloring and Dr. Vidal is in the office with him anyway."

She stood in front of her dad and made the most pleading look she could. She even tapped her toes and chanted, "Please, please, please."

She didn't expect it, but her dad nodded.

"Mandy, do you mind watching Edmund?" her dad yelled into the office.

"It would be my pleasure," Dr. Vidal's voice came sailing out.

"Thank you," her dad said, and motioned for Clarissa to follow him.

As they walked towards the stairwell, Clarissa felt excitement rush through her.

Dad was walking so fast, Clarissa almost had to run to keep up.

They went down the stairs and through a thick, wooden door. It was too heavy for Clarissa to pull it open. Dad had to help.

She could only see the first room in the dim lighting. She knew the dim was to protect the artifacts. There was a musty smell of old things, and bone dust in every breath she took. She put her hand around the key in her pocket. It felt comforting to hold it.

"Do not touch anything," her dad said. "It is very important."

A large rectangular structure covered by a blanket stood in the corner.

"Is that the mummy?" Clarissa asked with a shiver.

"Yes, but please stay away from it," Dad said.

She nodded. She didn't want to get close to the mummy.

"I'm going to look around," Dad said. "You stay here." He pointed to a chair by a wooden desk covered with books.

Now was her chance. She could tell Dad about Kurt and his enemies.

"Dad, I think I know—" Clarissa said.

"I forgot my glasses upstairs," Dad said. "I'll just run back to the office to get them."

"But wait, Dad…" Clarissa said.

But Dad was out the door. She was alone.

Suddenly the chilly air in the basement seemed colder. The blanket on the mummy case swayed. She hoped it was just the wind.

She edged away from the corner with the mummy case. She clenched her fist around the key and shivered.

The key reminded her of the tree. She felt better thinking about Oak. Soon, she would be safe in its twisty branches.

An orange light caught her eye. It was coming from the keyhole of an old, iron box on a low shelf.

She crept to the shelf and picked up the little box. It was heavy. The metal was thick and cool. There was a big keyhole on one side, and latches on the other three. She peered through the keyhole.

Warm air blew on her eye from inside the box.

The keyhole glowed orange.

Chapter Seven

ould the key fit in the iron box? Clarissa had to know.

Oak had said all keys opened doors. A box lid was like a door, a very small one. Where would it take her?

Or what would it let out?

Her hand shook as she placed the key in the keyhole. It was a perfect fit.

Too excited to be afraid, she turned the key and opened the box.

What she expected to find, she did not know. But what she did find was disappointing.

It was just a little candle.

It was weird that the candle was lit, though. Clarissa wondered how long a candle could stay lit. Years? Hundreds of years?

Suddenly the blanket over the mummy's case shivered. Clarissa jumped as wind blew through the room.

She almost shrieked when she noticed Dad by the door. Then Clarissa realized what happened. When he opened the door, he caused the wind. It wasn't a mummy or ghost. She felt silly for being afraid.

But Dad was angry, which made her tense.

"Clarissa Anne!" he said, his voice firm. "I told you not to touch anything. Why would you light a candle here?"

"The candle was already lit," Clarissa explained.

"What?" he said, and came close. "That's not possible." He put his finger to the flame and pulled back quickly, then sucked on his finger.

"It really was lit," she said. "The box was locked…I mean closed." She didn't want to say anything about her key. She wanted to be able to keep it.

"Fire needs oxygen to burn," he said. "The flame should have used up all the oxygen in this little box quickly. Then it should have gone out."

Clarissa's throat felt tight. Dad never believed her. It wasn't fair. After all, she told the truth.

He closed the box and the key stuck out of it.

"You will see this candle is out when I open the box again," her dad said. "And then you'll tell me why you lit this candle and where you got the match."

But when he opened the box, the candle was still lit.

And when he blew on the flame it did not go out. Clarissa thought it even burned brighter when he blew on it, as if it was angry.

"I swear I didn't light it," Clarissa said.

Dad's eyebrows pinched together.

"I am going to take a quick look around for the bottle," he said. "You will sit right there and not move or touch anything else."

She sank down on a cold, metal chair. It wasn't fair. Dad was angry that she lit the candle. But she didn't light it. He would never believe her.

Chin in hand, she stared at the flame in the box. It flickered.

The blanket on the mummy case was moving back and forth.

She shivered with cold and fear.

The flame did a weird thing, then. It grew longer and bent towards her.

She was about to move off the chair and go to the box when Dad came in.

"All right, no trace of the bottle," he said. "We'll take the box upstairs with us." He tried to blow the flame out again. A spark shot out and caught his sleeve.

Clarissa had the strange thought that the spark knew he was trying to blow it out. She was glad it fought back.

They left the spooky basement. Clarissa felt warmer as soon as they stepped into the hallway.

When they got to the office, Edmund was alone. Where was Dr. Vidal?

Edmund was standing up on Dad's chair. He picked a smooth stone off the woven basket on his desk. Clarissa watched in horror as he put the stone in his mouth.

"No, Edmund!" Dad ran to him. "Spit it out." But Edmund only gave a mighty swallow and reached for another.

Clarissa moved the basket away and searched her brother for signs of pain. Dad seemed to panic, walking back and forth across the office in jerky motions. He came to a sudden stop.

"We need to go to the hospital," Dad said. "Who knows how many he ate."

Edmund only smiled at them, so Clarissa wasn't too worried. But Dad gathered up his things and said they had to go right away. He forgot about the box, so Clarissa slipped the closed box with the lit candle into her bag.

A chill ran through her when she remembered what the tree told her.

A fire is coming. It will start with a girl and a key.

Chapter Eight

That evening was clear and bright. Stars were out. There was a crisp chill to the air.

Clarissa stood in front of the oak tree with the iron box in her hands. She waited for Oak to wake up. Usually it took seconds or minutes. But more and more, the tree kept sleeping.

The tree didn't answer her hellos. She sat on the dry ground and rested her back on the trunk. The moon rose above the flat horizon, a giant hot air balloon. She wished she could tie a basket to it and be carried up into the sky.

Clarissa fell asleep, sitting against the tree. She dreamt of being up high and chatting with the stars.

A leaf tickled her face and she woke up. Oak bent a branch down to her and was tickling her still.

"Stop," she said, giggling.

"Good evening, or is it morning, little one?" the oak tree spoke.

"It's evening," she said with a yawn. The moon was still low, so she knew she hadn't slept long.

"Then why are you waking up?" the tree said, and laughed a booming laugh. "Morning is for waking. Nighttime is for gazing at the stars." The tree stretched its branches high and wide.

The stars looked bigger than normal and twice as shiny.

"Do you see The Great Bear?" Oak said.

"I see the Plough," Clarissa said. "I think it's called The Big Dipper, too."

"The Plough is in The Great Bear," Oak said. "It has many names. The Saucepan might be my favorite."

Clarissa laughed.

"Mine too," she said. "Maybe the Great Bear is cooking something."

Oak rumbled a laugh, shaking its leaves.

"I spend more and more time looking at the stars these days," Oak said. "They are more wonderful to me with each passing moon. Just look how bright the North Star is tonight."

Clarissa suddenly remembered why she was there. The key, which she had dug up on the north side of the tree. She jumped to her feet, excited.

"Look what I found!" Clarissa said. "I opened it with the key you gave me."

She held the iron box out to the tree. The flame was burning, just as before.

"What is this?" Oak said. "That flame is old, very old."

"How do you know?" Clarissa asked. "How old is it?"

"As old as the key and older," Oak said. "I will need to talk to Willow about this."

"What do I do with it?" she asked.

"Do?" the tree asked. "Why do you need to do anything? Wait until we know more."

Clarissa closed the box.

She wasn't good at waiting.

The tree asked her where she found the box,

and she told the whole story of her day. She got to go into the museum basement after all. It was worth telling the tree all about that, so she did.

"I probably have bone dust in my hair," Clarissa said.

The tree pretended to sneeze by folding in its branches and then springing them out again and making a sound like, "Achoo."

She also told how her little brother ate at least one stone.

"Edmund's probably fine," Clarissa said. "The doctor said to watch for symptoms, and have dinner that's easy to digest. So, we're having rice pudding tonight."

"Hmmm," the tree made a deep, rattling sound and shook its leaves.

Oak said it was getting tired. It thanked her for her stories and told her to come back the next evening.

Dad was still cooking the rice pudding, so Clarissa hopped upstairs to her bedroom. She took out the special journal, the one with jasmine flowers on the cover.

Dear Mum,

You will never guess where I was allowed to go today. The museum basement! It was so exciting and kind of scary. Remember how you used to say Dad had bone dust in his hair? Well, I probably do too.

I can't wait to tell Preeti all about it, especially about the mummy in the corner.

Edmund ate a stone. But don't worry, he seems fine. I just showed Oak this flame in a box I opened with the key I told you about. Oak said it was an old and maybe important flame. But I'm not supposed to do anything with it. Waiting and not doing anything is so hard.

We're eating rice pudding tonight. I hope you are safe somewhere and maybe having something nice like rice pudding too. If you still eat.

Love you 'til the end of time,
Clarissa

Dad called her downstairs. Clarissa put the box with the flame in it into a bag and slung it over her shoulder. Just because Oak told her not to do anything with it didn't mean she couldn't keep it with her.

In the kitchen, she scooped out a big bowl of rice pudding. She went to the living room to eat it by the fire. The iron box was in her bag next to her. Edmund was happily slurping his food on the sofa. Dad's bowl was next to him and he was typing on his laptop from his armchair.

Everything seemed normal, except for Shadow. He wasn't curled up and asleep as usual. He was hissing at Clarissa's bag.

Chapter Nine

*W*hen Dad got up to go wash their bowls in the kitchen, Clarissa took out the iron box. Shadow hissed and arched his back as if he wanted to fight the box.

"Easy, boy," Clarissa said. She opened the box and the flame burned bright.

"What to do with you?" Clarissa asked the flame. She put the key in her pocket. Maybe she should return the box to the museum where it belonged. At least she could keep the key.

Shadow tried to get between the flame and Clarissa. But he was afraid of the fire, small though it was. Shadow ended up on her shoulder, with his furry body in her face.

Clarissa sneezed and the flame jumped. Shadow jumped off Clarissa and ran to Edmund on the sofa.

Clarissa put the box down to grab a tissue, and then a strange thing happened. The flame jumped again, higher. It landed in the fire.

Now the candle in the box was out. The log in the fireplace crackled, and the flames grew.

Clarissa's heart beat fast. Was the candle in the box broken?

"Ah," a voice from the fire said. "That is better."

Clarissa turned to see if anyone else heard the fire speak.

From the sofa, Shadow stared at the flames with yellow eyes. Edmund was staring at the fire in the exact same way, with blue eyes.

At least it wasn't just her who thought there was something strange about the fire.

"Did you…just speak?" she asked the fire.

"You are the girl who released me," the fire spoke in a crackling voice. "It is so good to be free again."

A shadow face with a dark mouth and two round, soot eyes formed with flames all around.

"Who…or what…are you?" she asked.

"I am an ancient fire spirit," it said. "Who and what are you?"

"I'm a girl," she said. She held up the iron box with the unlit candle.

"Do you live in this box?" she asked.

"I was most unfairly trapped in that box," it said, and the flames grew higher. Clarissa's face was burning hot and she scooted farther back.

"Now that you have released my heart flame, I am free again," it said. "I am connected to fire throughout the world. I stretch, and a volcano erupts in Hawaii. I crackle, and trees burn!"

"Oh no, don't burn the trees," Clarissa said. She had heard terrible stories of trees in the Amazon burning down, and all the birds and forest life losing their tree homes.

"But I am fire!" it said. "I live on wood like this log right here." Hot flames curled around the wood.

She suddenly felt afraid for their very own oak tree in the garden.

Edmund stayed on the sofa, still staring. But

Shadow found his courage and crept up to Clarissa's knee.

"There is much drought in the world now," the fire spoke. "It is much drier in places than when I was last released. So much more to burn!"

Clarissa thought fast. How could she convince the fire spirit not to go burning all the forests?

"It was a tree that released you, not me," Clarissa said. "It gave me the key."

The fire crackled lower and the shadow eyes grew larger.

"A tree?" the fire spirit said. "Why would a tree release me?"

"I don't know," Clarissa said. "It just did."

The flames burned lower, quieter.

"Never has a living tree been fire's friend," it said in a smaller voice. "You must be a powerful girl, to command a tree."

"Oak's my friend," Clarissa said. "It was Oak's idea to give me the key. I'm not powerful."

"You released me, an ancient and powerful fire spirit," it said. "You must have a strong and powerful flame inside you to do such a deed."

Clarissa didn't think she was powerful. She certainly didn't feel that way, curled up on a cushion on the floor. Heat from the flames baked her face and hands. The powerful one was definitely the fire. Not her.

"Bedtime, children," her dad came in with a tea towel over his shoulder. "Edmund, all good?"

Her brother nodded with glistening eyes and an open mouth. Clarissa knew that was his excited face. The last time he looked that way was when they watched the Avengers movie.

"No stomach pains?" her dad said, scooping Edmund up. He shook his head, still staring at the fire.

"Dad, look…" Clarissa said but the face in the flames was gone. The fire burned low.

Dad wasn't paying attention anyway. He carried her brother upstairs.

"Goodnight, fire," she said, and got up from the cushions to head to bed.

But the fire was silent.

She hoped it would speak to her again.

Chapter Ten

"Clarissa!" Her dad's voice reached into her dreams and pulled her out of sleep. She blinked at him. He came into focus.

"What?" she asked and rubbed her eyes. It was still dark. Her alarm clock read 6:14 a.m.

"The box with the lit candle is still in the office," he said, pulling his hair. "I forgot it there. The whole place could be burned down!"

Clarissa was so sleepy, but she tried hard to think. Should she tell him she had the box, and the candle was out? Dad would be angry that she took it from the museum.

And how could she explain about the fire spirit? Dad would never believe her.

"It was a trick, Dad," she said, making up a story. "A trick candle, but I put it out before we left your office. Sorry."

Her dad sat up straight. The look he gave her chilled her a little. She pulled her blanket up around her.

"That was a very silly trick," he said. "I expect you to be more mature than that."

"Sorry, it was only a joke," Clarissa said. Obviously she didn't play a trick on her dad. But she couldn't tell him that. He wouldn't believe the truth.

"You're doing the dishes tonight as punishment," he said.

"Okay," Clarissa said. Actually she didn't mind doing the dishes. She found it relaxing to soap up dishes and cups and wash them all clean. She wasn't going to tell Dad that, though.

"All right, I am relieved the candle is out," her dad said. He smoothed down his hair.

"Did you find the potion bottle?" Clarissa asked and propped herself up on the pillows.

Her dad nodded.

"Mandy, I mean Dr. Vidal, talked with Sophie, who had taken it home to clean it," he said.

Clarissa's surprise made her feel more awake. So, Kurt hadn't stolen the bottle after all.

"Clean it?" Clarissa said. "But there was potion in that bottle. Sophie didn't empty it, did she?"

Clarissa remembered the little red bottle had liquid in it. She remembered how Kurt opened the stopper and smelled it.

"I certainly hope Sophie didn't open the bottle," he said. "But she's already broken a rule. No items should be removed from the museum!"

Clarissa felt a little guilty that the iron box, which should be in the basement, was in their house. But it could not be helped.

Maybe she could find a way to get the iron box back where it belonged.

"Um, could I come with you to the museum basement again?" she asked. She hoped to put the box back where she found it, before Dad could discover it and get mad.

"I need to go in later today," he said.

"On Sunday?" Clarissa asked.

"Would you like to come with me?" he said. "Maybe Edmund would like to see the basement too."

Clarissa froze inside. It was a cold anger that filled her. She had begged to go to the basement all her life and she had to wait until she was eleven. Now Edmund got to go and he wasn't even three.

She didn't know what to say. She just curled her arms around her knees and hugged herself.

"All right, kiddo," he said. "Go back to sleep. It's still early. I know I could use a few more hours. Pancakes later."

He kissed her forehead and went back to his room. But she was too angry to sleep. Anyway, he burned pancakes when he tried to make them. She was not looking forward to black pancakes.

She did not want to lie in bed while she felt so awake. What she needed was to talk to Oak. So, she put on her comfortable hooded sweatshirt and padded down the stairs. Shadow meowed when he saw her and brushed against her pajamas.

While she was petting him, she heard something. It sounded like, "girl."

It was coming from the direction of the fireplace. The fire had gone out. She poked the blackened log and embers glowed.

Girl. Clarissa heard a weak whisper.

She knew how to light a fire. Dad had taught her. She pulled out the pine wood logs and stacked them in a pyramid. Thin sticks and newspaper went under the pyramid.

The newspaper caught on the embers. Soon, she had a fire roaring.

The face in the flames came back.

"Thank you, girl," it said. "Or do you have a name?"

"I'm Clarissa," she answered. "What's your name?"

"You can call me Fire," it said.

"Since you released me, the old code requires that I repay you," Fire said. "And I need to repay the tree who helped free me."

"Repay us…how?" Clarissa asked.

"Name your price," Fire said.

Chapter Eleven

Clarissa could think of many things she wanted. She wanted to climb the spelling ladder again at school. She wanted her wooden dragonfly to be fixed.

"My teacher thinks I'm not doing well at school, but I am," Clarissa said. "I know the answers, I just don't say them."

"Do you wish me to frighten your teacher with flames?" Yellow sparks shot up into the chimney.

"Oh no, nothing like that," she said. "I just want her to know I'm studying and everything."

The fire made a humming noise.

"Can't you just tell her?" Fire asked. "This does

not sound like a price worthy of a fire spirit."

"My friend Preeti says I should answer more questions in class," Clarissa said.

The fire shot a bright spark upwards.

"You must speak your truth and flame bright," Fire said. "This is what my parent taught me."

Clarissa had never thought of herself as a flame. When she thought about answering a question in the middle of class, she felt more like a pond. Wet and wanting to hide deep under.

"Maybe I'm water, not fire," Clarissa said.

"Hmm, let me see," Fire said.

She felt heat, not just on her face, but all over her body. It was a warm and comfortable air-hug.

The heat left her.

"I sense much fire in you, little flame," Fire said. "So, you must find it and blaze as you should."

"Can you help me blaze?" Clarissa asked.

"Is that your price?" Fire asked.

What good would it do if Clarissa answered more questions? Really, that was just a school problem. When she thought about it, she had a bigger problem.

She met eyes with Shadow, who was watching from the sofa at the back of the room.

"Shadow remembers," Clarissa told Fire. "Dad used to be different. He doesn't talk and joke with me anymore."

She wanted Dad to spend time with her. These days, he just worked and took care of Edmund.

But Fire only said she should speak her truth to him and fan her flame.

"How can I speak my truth if he won't listen?" Clarissa asked.

"Blaze brighter," Fire said.

Clarissa felt tired. She didn't think she could talk normally to Dad ever again.

"Look, if you can't help me with my problem, what can you give me as a price?" she asked.

"I can burn villages," Fire said. "I can destroy houses and forests."

Clarissa didn't want anything to burn, though.

"Can you do anything good?" she asked.

"What does that mean?" Fire asked.

"You know, something that helps people," Clarissa said.

The fire crackled steadily. Yellow sparks shot up the chimney.

"Ah," the face in the flames said. "My parent once took me to a temple when I was just a little flame. We burned in ever-lit candles for days.

"The holy people talked about good action instead of bad," Fire said. "I listened to the chants, but I am fire. I do not do good or bad. I just burn things."

"Isn't burning bad?" she asked.

"No," Fire said.

Clarissa wasn't sure about that. It sounded awfully bad to her to burn forests and start volcanoes. She said so.

"Hot lava deep in the Earth's core called magma is at the very center of our planet," Fire said. "It needs to be fiery. I visited it while you slept. Ah, it was so warm and molten!

"During your sleep, I journeyed to three volcanoes deep under the ocean and awakened them," the shadow face in the flames said. "You may say that is bad, but those volcanoes that erupted will one day become new islands on top of the water. Life will grow in the new islands."

"So...we need fire," Clarissa said. "And volcanoes."

"I also spied on many humans through their fireplaces," it said. "Maybe that was bad behavior." The fire flickered and yellow sparks shot up.

"It must be nice to travel around to so many places," Clarissa said. "I would like to do that."

"Is that your price for freeing me?" Fire asked. "I can help you travel in a big hot air balloon."

That sounded fun. But could she really leave Edmund alone? Dad would take care of him, but Dad also worked hard and didn't have enough time.

If she left, who would tell Edmund stories about Mum?

She only got one price—one wish. She wanted to think about it and talk it over with the tree.

"I need to think about my price," Clarissa said.

"Very well," Fire said. "While I wait I will enjoy going everywhere. It is awesome to spread my flames throughout the world. Thanks to you and the oak tree, I am truly free."

"You can come here anytime," Clarissa said. "We almost always have a fire here, especially now that it's autumn."

The fire turned orange and grew larger.

"Fire has no home," it said. "Though your offer is kind."

Clarissa's stomach rumbled. She was hungry, but remembered Dad was making burnt pancakes later. She sighed.

Fire asked what was the matter, and she explained both the hunger and the pancakes.

"I can help you make pancakes," Fire said.

"You can cook?"

"I am fire—of course I can cook," Fire said.

Clarissa leapt up. She ran to the kitchen and turned on all four gas burners.

"Why are you in here?" Fire said through the flames on the stovetop. Now its voice was high and whiny. But she could hear it clearly.

"This is the kitchen," Clarissa said.

"When I last flamed in the world, people cooked over the hearth fire," the little voice said.

"Is the hearth fire the one in the living room?" Clarissa asked.

"Yes, the big fire," it said.

"Oh," Clarissa said. "Now we have kitchens and these smaller flames."

"The world has changed so much. If you insist on these small flames, I suppose I can work with it. Find a flat pan," the squeaky voice said. "And a bowl, and milk and flour…"

Fire told her the ingredients in no particular order. She managed to put something together that looked like batter. He told her just how to grease the pan, then add the batter carefully with a big spoon. Soon, the smell of pancakes–yummy, unburned pancakes–filled the kitchen.

When she was finished, a stack of funny-looking pancakes stood tall on a plate. The last one was perfectly round. The fire congratulated her on it.

Clarissa's sweatshirt was covered in flour. A lump of batter was stuck in her long ponytail. She laughed.

Her dad walked in and stood at the doorway to the kitchen, blinking at her. Clarissa held up the plate of pancakes and smiled with joy.

"You look just like your mum," he said. "It smells like you can cook as well as your mum too. Where did you learn to make those?"

Clarissa just kept smiling.

What could she say?

A fire spirit taught her.

Chapter Twelve

They didn't go to Dad's office in the end. Edmund had a stomachache, so they all stayed home. Dad worried it was the stone he ate, but Clarissa thought it was because he ate ten pancakes.

It was a gray Sunday morning. Instead of playing board games in bed, like they used to do with Mum, they were all in the living room doing their own thing.

It was hard to believe Dad ever played board games.

They all sat in their usual places in the living room. Dad was on his armchair and Edmund was on the sofa. Shadow visited each one of them in turn, and was sitting by Clarissa's leg at the moment. She sat on the floor, nearest the fire.

The fireplace held just a normal fire. There was no face in the flames.

Clarissa wondered where the fire spirit went. Probably somewhere exciting like a volcano in Hawaii.

It was finally raining. Dad said it was a blessing, because it hadn't rained in weeks and it was good for the garden. But the rain annoyed her. She needed to talk to the Oak and ask its price for freeing the fire spirit. But she didn't feel like getting wet.

She shifted on her cushions and let out an annoyed "argh" sound, which startled Shadow.

Maybe she would feel better if she talked to Mum.

She headed upstairs and flopped on her bed. She opened her special journal with jasmine flowers on it.

Dear Mum,

It's Sunday morning. Are you playing board games? Dad stopped doing that. I miss it. Preeti plays games with her brothers. But Edmund is too small to play with me. So I have no one to play with. Oh well.

I want to tell you something important. I opened an old box and let a fire spirit free. It lives in our fireplace sometimes and talks to me. Edmund can see it, and Shadow too. It doesn't come if Dad is around.

The fire spirit helped me make pancakes like you used to make. They were pretty good.

Mum, are fire spirits good or bad?

I know you can't answer. But maybe you can send me a sign.

Love you 'til the end of time,
Clarissa

She finished writing and put the journal in the drawer of her bedside table. A thrill ran through her when she saw the rain had stopped. Maybe Oak was awake. She really wanted to tell it all about the fire spirit.

Oak was awake and shook its leaves with happiness when she came near.

"Hello, child," Oak said. "Ah, the rain was delicious." It stretched its branches to the sky.

"I stayed inside, dry," Clarissa said. "And guess what? The fire spirit helped me make pancakes!"

"The fire spirit?" the tree asked.

"It visits me in the fireplace," she said. "I know you told me not to do anything with the flame in the box. It jumped on its own."

She told the tree how the little flame in the box leapt into the fire and talked to her.

"I knew that flame was old and alive," the tree said. "Willow said it could be a lost fire spirit who visited us a long time ago."

Oak stretched its branches high and shook them in a show of excitement.

"This could be good for our land, if it is not angry," Oak said. "Is it?"

"The fire spirit says since you helped me free it, you can ask for a price," she said. "It doesn't seem angry."

"Ah, so it is a friend," Oak said. "This is verrrrrry good." The tree made the 'r' last long. The sound echoed through its trunk.

"I know my wish," Oak said and shook its branches hard. "Tell the fire to bring back the wisps."

"The will-o'-the-wisps you told me about?" she asked.

"Yes, the little flames that float in the air and guide lost travelers at night," Oak said. "I miss them. They were good for our land."

"Weren't some of them bad—they led people the wrong way?" Clarissa asked, remembering the oak tree's stories.

"You can try to tell the fire spirit to bring back good wisps," the tree said. "But the wisps have a mind of their own."

"Is fire bad?" Clarissa asked. "You know, because it burns down forests and makes volcanoes erupt and things?"

The tree was quiet for a minute. Then it made a deep, humming noise as if it were clearing its throat.

"Sometimes, little one, it is time for great change," the tree said. "With change there can come destruction. And then new growth."

"Like a new island after a volcano erupts?" she asked.

"Exactly," the tree said.

"When Edmund was born…well, you know, you were there," Clarissa said.

"Tell me," the tree said.

"Well, Mum died," she said. "Is that like… destruction, and then new growth?" Clarissa asked.

"Yes, though that was very sad, of course," the tree said. A branch came down to rest on her shoulder.

"I think it's bad she died," Clarissa said. "I want her back."

"It is neither bad nor good," Oak said. "It is just the way things are." Oak placed a woven crown onto her hair.

"Wow, what's this?" she asked.

"A gift from Willow," the tree said.

"Should I go thank her?" Clarissa asked.

"She is a little afraid of humans," Oak said. "She likes you, so you can wave to her from here. That would be best."

Clarissa thanked Willow, and skipped inside the house wearing her new crown. She couldn't wait to ask the fire spirit to bring back helpful wisps.

Dad didn't look up from his laptop when Clarissa came into the living room. Edmund looked at the top of her head with his mouth in an 'O' of excitement. She guessed he liked the willow crown. She took it off and carefully placed it on his head. He smiled his biggest smile.

She sank down and stared into the faceless flames. The tree knew what it wanted.

What did she want?

What she really wanted deep down was to have things go back to the way they were before. When Dad used to listen to her and didn't ignore her.

She knew Mum was gone and couldn't come back. But in a way, Dad was gone, too.

Could he come back?

Chapter Thirteen

Clarissa stared into the crackling red and orange flames.

Maybe the fire spirit was right. It said to speak her truth and fan her flame.

A blackened log showed hot orange where the fire was. The black part wouldn't burn anymore. It was ash. But there were still orange parts, hot and fiery. Maybe Dad wasn't a dead, black part. Maybe the fire was still there.

She would blaze bright.

Dad was typing on his laptop when she came up next to him, her hands on her hips.

"Dad," she said, in a strong voice.

Dad didn't look up, but stared at his laptop screen.

"Honey, I don't have time just now," he said, waving her away with one hand. "Sophie says she didn't take the medieval potion."

Clarissa could see this was no time for a conversation about being fun Dad again. She sighed a deep sigh.

"Dr. Vidal said Sophie took the potion," Clarissa said.

He pulled at his hair as he picked up his cell phone.

"I just got an email from Sophie saying she didn't take it," he said. "I'm going to call her."

Curiosity turned Clarissa's thoughts to the potion mystery.

Did Dr. Vidal lie about Sophie taking the potion?

Was she covering for her boyfriend Kurt?

The image of the silver bracelet with the charm shaped like a love potion swam into her mind.

Was Dr. Vidal under Kurt's spell?

"Dad, Kurt was really interested in the potion," Clarissa said. But her dad made a shushing noise and leaned closer to his laptop.

Clarissa crossed her arms.

"Dad, I just know Kurt took the potion," Clarissa said, a little louder this time. Shadow peered at her with his ears pricked. Edmund stared from the sofa, a crayon in his hand.

"Sophie's number is 897 422," Dad said to his laptop. He pulled out his phone.

Clarissa's face grew hot. She had a yell inside her, but it didn't come out.

She would tell the fire spirit that she tried to speak her truth, but Dad wouldn't listen. Not even to the important fact that Kurt was interested in the potion at the museum. Kurt even opened the bottle and smelled it.

Dr. Vidal had said Kurt had enemies. He could use a fire spirit to protect himself.

Too bad Dad wouldn't listen to her. He was missing important clues.

Dad got up from his comfortable armchair and walked into the kitchen with his phone to his ear.

He said, "Hello, Sophie." Then his voice was too low to hear anything else.

Clarissa went back to her floor cushions and plopped down. She buried her face in her hands. She felt a lick on her ankle and peeked through her hands to see Shadow.

At least Shadow still loved her.

Clarissa's shoulders slumped. Dad would never go back to normal, never play games in bed on Sunday morning.

A *whoosh* from the fireplace made her jump.

"Eeee!" Clarissa shouted. The flames had a face.

Shadow danced backwards to the end of the room and jumped onto the sofa. Edmund blinked at the fire. Shadow crawled into his lap.

Clarissa knelt as close to the fire as she could, feeling the heat on her face.

"Girl, will you name your price?" the face in the flames said.

But Clarissa had questions.

"Why won't you show yourself when Dad is here?" Clarissa asked.

"I trust very few humans," Fire said.

"Where did you go this time?" she asked Fire.

Yellow sparks jumped up into the chimney.

"I journeyed far," Fire said. "It felt so good to stretch my flames."

The fire spirit had visited a place deep under the sea, called the Mariana Trench. Giant tube worms lived in hot vents there. Clarissa thought it would be wonderful to visit deep under the sea. Starfish, whales and oysters were things she wanted to see. Maybe not giant tube-worms, though.

"You must choose your price," Fire said. "I feel a heaviness in me. I have not repaid you or the tree. I must come back here again and again until I pay."

"I don't know my price," Clarissa said. "But the oak tree wants you to bring back the will-o'-the-wisps."

The flames became smaller and the fire spirit's voice was quiet.

"I will not pay that price," it said.

"Why can't you do it?" she said. "You're a fire spirit."

"I didn't say I couldn't do it," Fire said. "But I won't."

"Why not?"

"It is how I got captured in the first place, doomed to spend a hundred years in that tiny box," it said. Yellow flames licked upwards. "Fire spirits are supposed to roam the world, not live in a box."

Its voice was loud. Clarissa twisted around to see if Edmund was listening. But he had gone back to sleep. Shadow sat on top of him and watched the flames with steady eyes.

The fire spirit explained that to make wisps, it had to use its heart flame. A heart flame was small and could be captured. Or worse, it could be put out.

"If my heart flame was put out, I would die," Fire said. "I would become a star." Its shadow eyes grew bigger.

"But you can be careful," Clarissa said. "Make good will-o'-the-wisps that help people, so no one would want to put your heart flame out."

"I trust you, and I speak to you with my heart flame," it said. "If you threw water on me now, though, I would die. So, I am very careful who I speak to."

"My mum died," Clarissa said. "I don't want you to die. Dying is forever."

"Yes, a black log turned to ash," Fire said.

"That's what I think too," Clarissa said.

The fire turned orange. Clarissa felt a gentle warmth on her face and hands.

"My parent died," it said. "We fire spirits just have one parent. Mine died and became a star, like all fire spirits become at the end."

"I'm sorry," Clarissa said. "Can't you bring your parent back?"

"I cannot bring back the dead," it said.

"You can't bring back wisps," Clarissa said, feeling a spark of anger run through her. "You can't bring back the dead. What can you do?"

"Well, little flame," Fire said, yellow sparks shooting up. "I am sorry to disappoint you. But I can tell you one thing."

"What?" Clarissa said, her arms crossed fiercely over her chest.

"I can tell you where the lost potion is," Fire said.

Chapter Fourteen

The wood shifted in the fireplace with a clunk as it burned. Clarissa came closer to the flames. Heat baked into her face and hands. The face made of fire stared back at her with black, shadow eyes.

"How do you know about the lost potion?" Clarissa asked.

"Though I do not show myself, I listen from the hearth fire sometimes," Fire said.

"Dad thinks Sophie took the potion," Clarissa said softly. "But I think Kurt stole it."

"I do not know who Sophie or Kurt is," Fire said. "The potion calls me now. I know where it is."

"What do you mean, the potion calls you?" Clarissa asked.

"Two humans are trying to do a fire ceremony with the potion, to call and trap me," Fire said. "They are doing it wrong. I am very angry at them."

"Two people?" Clarissa asked. "Can you see anything more about them?"

"Let me see," Fire said. The flames lessened and the face disappeared. She guessed the fire spirit was travelling again.

After a few minutes, the flames roared and the shadow eyes and mouth returned to the fire.

"I see a man and a woman," Fire said. "The woman is under a spell. That is all I can see without jumping into their fire with my heart flame."

"I knew Dr. Vidal was under a spell!" Clarissa said. "I'm sure it's that charm bracelet Kurt gave her. It has a charm on it that looks like a love potion."

"Charm or no charm, I am angry," Fire said. "They are trying to bring me to their fire."

"Is there a danger they will trap you?" Clarissa said, her hands sweating.

"Only if they do the ceremony correctly," Fire spoke. "But I will stop it soon. I am ready."

"Ready for what?" Clarissa asked.

"To jump in with the strongest, fiercest flame and burn them up," Fire said. "I will go when the rain stops."

A light drizzle pattered against the windows. Clarissa shivered despite the heat of the fire. She didn't want the fire spirit to burn up any people.

Dad had to hear this. Maybe he could stop the ceremony. But how could she make Dad believe any of it?

"Will you talk to Dad?" Clarissa said.

"No," Fire said. "I do not trust human adults."

"Can you tell me where the potion is? Anything at all?" she asked.

The flames lessened as the face in the flames disappeared. The fire spirit was travelling again.

Soon, the fire spirit was back and the fire was roaring.

"The fire ceremony is outside, not far from here. It is near a great curve in the river," the flames said. "There are weeds, grass and willow trees. I can burn the trees. A large metal building stands near, not good for burning."

A picture formed in Clarissa's mind. She knew where that was.

She could bike there. But she was afraid to go on her own.

"When the rain stops, I will go and burn the fire strong and bright," Fire said with a roar. "The humans and the potion will be no more."

Flames shot up the chimney.

"Please don't hurt anyone," Clarissa said. "Dad and I can get the potion peacefully."

"Fire burns, that's what I do," Fire said. "Destruction gives rise to new life when fire is done. That is the cycle of things."

Water streamed down the window. But how long would it keep raining?

Dad could drive her to the place by the river in five minutes. How could she convince him?

While she was thinking about it, her father came downstairs. He rushed through the living room to the hall by the front door. Shadow meowed at him loudly.

She tried to talk to him as he pulled on his raincoat. Shadow was getting under his feet.

"Dad, I think I know where the potion—" Clarissa started, but he cut her off.

"I just spoke to Sophie," Dad said. He pulled on his shoes and shook Shadow off one. "She says Dr. Vidal never called her in the first place. Now I don't know who to believe."

He grabbed his keys from the hook by the door and walked out.

"Dad, I think Kurt—" Clarissa shouted to Dad from the doorway.

But her dad talked over her.

"Mrs. Beech is coming over to watch you and Edmund," he said and opened the car door. "I'm going to the police station in town."

Dad waved at something across the street. Mrs. Beech, their neighbor, was making her way towards the house.

"But Dad, I need to talk to you!" Clarissa yelled.

"Later," Dad said. He closed the car door and started the engine.

Shadow meowed at her sadly as Clarissa slumped against the doorframe. With Dad gone, what could she do now?

She started walking to the oak tree to ask its advice, but Mrs. Beech ushered her inside before she could get there.

"Darling, it is very wet," her kind, gray-haired neighbor said. "Get inside and I'll make us all hot cocoa."

Clarissa let Mrs. Beech lead her into the house. The rain pattered steadily, but it could end any minute. Clarissa knew she had to stop the ceremony before it stopped raining.

She had to get there before the angry fire spirit did.

Chapter Fifteen

Clarissa's hot cocoa sat untouched by her knee. She didn't feel like drinking it. Now that Dad was driving to his office, and wouldn't help, it was down to her to stop the ceremony.

How could she leave the house without Mrs. Beech knowing?

Maybe it would help to write to Mum. After all, if she did go to the ceremony and something went terribly wrong, someone should know where she was.

Dear Mum,

I am sorry if my writing is messy. My knee is bouncing up and down. I need to leave the house, but Mrs. Beech is downstairs.

Two people are trying to trap the fire spirit in a ceremony. I think they are Kurt and Dr. Vidal. Dr. Vidal is under a love spell that makes her lie for Kurt. It's sad because she used to be honest and good. Even though she always did hug way too tight.

The fire spirit wants to burn up the potion, the trees and the people as soon as it stops raining. I can't let it do that.

Dad won't listen to me. I'm pretty sure I know where they are—near the asphalt plant by the river. So I am going to go stop the ceremony before the fire spirit gets there.

Fire says when fire spirits die they become stars. Mum, are you a star? I think you are, and that you've watching us from the sky. That means dying isn't forever, it's just a big change. Destruction giving rise to new life, like the fire spirit says.

It's cool if you're a star. I'm going now, to try to stop anyone from getting hurt. I hope you will help, from all the way up there in the sky.

Wish me luck.
Love you 'til the end of time,
Clarissa

She felt better having told her plan to Mum. She smelled potatoes and herbs. Mrs. Beech must be in the kitchen cooking.

Maybe now she could sneak out.

The fire spirit was humming in the fireplace. She heard it as she crept down the stairs. It was a good sign. The fire spirit would hide if Mrs. Beech were in the living room.

Edmund and Shadow were on the sofa, and the fire spirit threw a spark her way. The clattering of pots and pans came from the kitchen.

Clarissa waved to the fire spirit. She didn't share her plan to save the potion and people. She didn't want the fire spirit to go early and burn everything up.

Hopefully she'd be able to stop the fire ceremony before the fire spirit got there.

As a goodbye, she kissed her little brother's forehead. He just watched her silently from his cocoon in the blankets.

Shadow meowed at her, his yellow eyes large. Clarissa tensed as she pulled on her raincoat. Shadow's meowing might give her away. She hoped Mrs. Beech would not come to see what the trouble was. Clarissa slipped out the door.

The rain was much lighter now.

Before getting on her bike, she tried to wake Oak and tell it her plan. It might have a good idea how to stop the ceremony.

But Oak wouldn't talk or move. So, she jumped on her bike and pedaled in the light rain towards the river.

Her face was wet, but her hood kept the rain off well enough, so she could see. It didn't take long to get to the river. She turned onto the muddy path and biked along the water.

The weather was too wet for most people to be out. The path was almost empty. She could bike fast. It wasn't long before she smelled burning wood and saw a column of smoke.

The rain was thin enough to allow the smoke to show against the sky.

When she got nearer, she heard chanting.

Her heart sank.

Dr. Vidal and Kurt were sitting across from each other, with a fire in between. The fire was still just a low, smoldering campfire. The fire spirit hadn't come yet.

A box of firelighters was sitting close to the flames. Clarissa felt her heart tighten. Everyone knew not to have firelighters near a fire.

Dr. Vidal and Kurt were both chanting.

Kurt held a little red bottle. Smoke curled around it.

Clarissa rested her bike on a tree trunk. She hoped the smoke wasn't damaging the bottle. It was a museum item, after all.

Dr. Vidal and Kurt weren't paying attention to her. They were looking into the fire and chanting.

Clarissa would have to use her voice. She cleared her throat.

"Fan your flame," she whispered to herself.

She took a deep, brave breath in.

"Dr. Vidal!" Clarissa yelled out. "Take off your charm bracelet and stop what you're doing!"

"Clarissa?" Dr. Vidal stood up. She wore a tan jacket, her dark hair hanging loose. Her face was painted with red and black markings. Dr. Vidal and

Kurt were wearing face paint just like in ancient ceremonies

"Who is that girl?" said the man with similar face paint. "She shouldn't be here."

"It's Clarissa. I know her," Dr. Vidal said. "Clarissa, never mind what we're doing. Go home."

"I know exactly what you are doing!" Clarissa said. "You are trying to call the fire spirit, so you can trap him. Well guess what? The fire spirit doesn't want to be trapped!"

Both Dr. Vidal and Kurt stared at Clarissa. Kurt stood up. He was very tall, and Clarissa was scared.

But she would be brave and fan her flame, like the fire spirit said.

"Dr. Vidal, he's put you under a spell," Clarissa shouted. "Take off the love charm!"

"It is no love spell," Kurt said. "The bracelet was a gift from my heart to yours."

Dr. Vidal raised her wrist to her eyes and examined it.

"The charm does look like a love potion," Dr. Vidal said. "Strange…but Kurt would never do such a thing." She batted her eyelashes at her boyfriend.

Then Clarissa noticed something that scared her even more. The rain had stopped. That meant the fire spirit was coming to burn up everything and everyone.

The fire roared and sparks jumped out of it. The adults jumped back. The face in the fire was huge, bigger than Clarissa had ever seen it. Two shadow eyes in the flames were level with Dr. Vidal's eyes, and the mouth was down near her feet.

Dr. Vidal trembled and stared at the giant fire face. While she was distracted, Clarissa ran to her and quickly undid the charm bracelet.

Dr. Vidal sank to her knees, shaking.

Had her spell been lifted? Or was Dr. Vidal just scared?

"You dare call me?" the fire spirit said in a loud voice. It roared like a lion.

"It worked!" Kurt said, laughing and clapping his hands to the sky. "Quick, Mandy, the binding chant."

Clarissa tensed as Kurt poured the potion in the fire.

Would the fire spirit be trapped?

Chapter Sixteen

Clarissa stood as close to the roaring fire as she could. Oven-hot heat poured over the front of her body. Her face felt like a desert must feel. She coughed at a sudden wave of smoke.

"Fire spirit!" Clarissa yelled, coughing.

The face in the flames turned to her. The shadow eyes got bigger.

"Little flame," Fire said in a voice so loud Clarissa's eardrums shook. "Why are you here?"

"You said I need to speak my truth," Clarissa said. "To fan my flame. Well, I want you to stop. Don't hurt anyone."

"These human adults tried to capture me," Fire said. "I am angry."

"Listen to Clarissa," Dr. Vidal said as she moved away from the fire towards the river. "We're sorry. We won't do it again."

Clarissa felt a light of hope within her. Was Dr. Vidal back to her normal self?

"We are not sorry!" Kurt yelled. "You are our prisoner. You must do our bidding!"

"Ha!" Fire laughed. "You have not trapped me!" A flame licked out and zapped Kurt on his hand like a lightening bolt.

"Ouch!" Kurt rubbed his hand.

"I can do much worse," Fire said. "I WILL do much worse."

"Don't!" Clarissa said, her heart pounding hard. She was so hot inside her puffy coat. Sweat ran down her body. But she didn't want to move from the fire.

"Please don't hurt them or kill them," Clarissa said. "Because killing is forever. They'll be gone forever." Tears mixed with the sweat on her face.

"Little flame," Fire said in a softer voice. "Don't cry."

"My price for freeing you is not to hurt them," Clarissa said.

The shadow eyes looked at Clarissa for a few silent minutes.

"Very well, little flame," it finally said. The face in the flames grew smaller. The eyes and mouth shrank to tiny circles and then disappeared.

The fire spirit was gone. Burnt grass ringed the campfire. She placed her hand on the ground. It was dry.

The fire spirit had dried everything around it with its powerful flames.

"Why did you send the fire spirit away?" Kurt said in a loud voice, though nowhere near as loud as the fire spirit. He stepped towards Clarissa.

"You should not trap fire spirits," Clarissa said, her hands on her hips. "Fire needs to roam free."

Kurt stared at Clarissa looking surprised.

"First the little girl lets the fire spirit go, now she is yelling at me," Kurt said to Dr. Vidal. "Mandy, take her away before I get angrier."

Kurt was tall, but Clarissa wasn't scared. She had just stood up to a fire spirit after all. She kept her hands on her hips.

"Please, Kurt," Dr. Vidal said. "Clarissa saved our lives. That thing was big and scary."

"Why are you arguing?" Kurt said. "You are supposed to always agree with me." He grabbed her wrist and pushed the sleeve of her jacket up.

"Are you looking for the bracelet?" Dr. Vidal said.

"Where is it?" Kurt said.

"You should never have used magic on her," Clarissa yelled, holding up the bracelet.

"Put the bracelet back on, honey," Kurt said to Dr. Vidal. "We're a great team."

Dr. Vidal took the bracelet from Clarissa's small hand.

"I'm finally thinking clearly," Dr. Vidal said. "You're a thief and a liar. And you're playing with magic much too powerful than you can handle."

Dr. Vidal flung the bracelet into the river.

"You never loved me!" Dr. Vidal yelled.

At that moment, the wind started up. A whoosh and flash of light caught her eye.

The low campfire was roaring high again. Was the fire spirit back?

There was no face in the flames, and no voice coming from the fire. Instead, the box of firelighters was burning.

Clarissa's whole chest tightened with fear. The wind picked up the burning box of firelighters and lifted it into the hedge near the fire. The flames from the box licked up.

The wind blew smoke into her eyes. It stung.

Dead branches hanging down from a willow tree caught fire.

"We need to call someone!" Clarissa yelled and coughed at the smoke. She had no idea how far the fire could spread.

"Let's go," Kurt said and tugged Dr. Vidal's sleeve. "I have another bracelet at home…dear."

"No, I'm going to act responsibly for once," Dr. Vidal said. "I'll call the fire department." She took out her phone.

"Hello, we have a fire raging and a willow tree has caught fire," Dr. Vidal shouted into the phone. She gave their location and hung up.

"Clarissa," Dr. Vidal said. "I'm so sorry." She came over to Clarissa, and looked at her with big, brown eyes.

Kurt was running away, down the river.

The willow tree kept burning, the flames climbing higher. Clarissa prayed for it to be OK. She asked Mum to keep watch over it from the sky.

Dr. Vidal stood with Clarissa.

Sirens approached. The willow tree was still burning. Clarissa prayed it wouldn't die.

Dying was forever.

Dr. Vidal stayed by Clarissa as the sirens grew so loud she had to stick her fingers in her ears.

The fire truck had a huge hose on it. Two firemen jumped out and aimed the hose at the willow tree. A giant gush of water came out. It fell on the willow tree, beating back the flames.

Clarissa hoped the tree would be OK.

A police car drove up. Clarissa sort of hoped Dr. Vidal would get some punishment for what she did. Though she hoped it wouldn't be too bad.

Even though she hugged too tight, Clarissa kind of liked Dr. Vidal when she was nice.

But Kurt had run away.

That wasn't fair.

He shouldn't get away with what he did.

Clarissa felt the heat of anger in her cheeks.

Not only had Kurt stolen the potion bottle from the museum he had tried to trap a fire spirit.

A fire spirit, which was meant to roam free.

Chapter Seventeen

The fire was totally out. The grass and the willow tree were charred in places—black.

Dr. Vidal put one arm around Clarissa. Rose perfume filled Clarissa's senses. It tickled her throat and she coughed.

Dr. Vidal put the little empty bottle of potion into Clarissa's hand. The glass was smooth and cool.

"I should never have let him take this," Dr. Vidal said.

"It wasn't your fault," Clarissa said, coughing. "You were under a spell."

"Not at first," Dr. Vidal said, blinking. "From the beginning, he talked about using magic against other people. I should have never have gotten involved with him."

A policewoman came up to Dr. Vidal and Clarissa, asking what happened. It was too hard to explain, so Clarissa didn't say anything. Besides that, she kept coughing.

The policewoman asked Clarissa for her parents' phone number. Between coughs, she said Dad's number.

She hoped Dad wouldn't be too angry at her.

He would never understand about the fire spirit.

The policewoman took Dr. Vidal near the police car and pulled out a pad of paper. Clarissa was too far away to hear them. She was on her own for a minute.

Could she get on her bike and go home? The thought filled her with happiness.

Just like fire, she wanted to be free.

As she turned, a woman wearing a fluorescent jacket came up to her. She explained she was with emergency services and asked her to open her mouth. Clarissa did, trying not to cough with her mouth wide open. The woman asked her if it hurt anywhere, but it didn't.

The emergency services woman said it was luck Clarissa hadn't been burned at all. Clarissa was prescribed water and ice cream for her throat. The woman gave her a water bottle, but not ice cream, unfortunately.

She hoped once Dad forgave her he would allow her lots of ice cream.

Just as she was thinking that, Clarissa was grabbed and hugged again, but not too tight—just right. She recognized the green shirt her face pressed into.

It was Dad. When he let her go, he met her eyes. His were wild.

"Dad, you look…weird," Clarissa said between coughs.

"I was so worried!" he said, talking a mile a minute. "Why are you here? Where is Mrs. Beech?"

"I know I'm not supposed to—I left without telling her," she said. "I just had to stop the ceremony."

Dad looked over her head. Clarissa turned to see Dr. Vidal crying as she spoke with the policewoman.

Clarissa handed Dad the little, red bottle.

"Is that…the potion bottle?" her Dad said, taking the item. "I hope you know you are much more precious than this bottle."

Clarissa felt her eyes tear. Dad's words melted her heart and stung at the same time.

"Dr. Vidal and Kurt stole the potion," she said. "I tried to tell you but you wouldn't listen."

"I'm so sorry," he said. "How did you know they were here—did you follow them?"

Clarissa could have just said yes. She could have lied and made up a story.

But the fire spirit told her to speak her truth, to fan her flame.

So, she took a deep breath in and said, "Remember the box with the little candle that I said was a trick candle? Well, it was actually a fire spirit."

Dad blinked at her like he thought she was crazy but she kept telling her story. She got it all out - how Kurt was admiring the potions at the museum. How Dr. Vidal was under a love spell. How the fire spirit knew where the ceremony was and told her how to get here.

The only thing she didn't tell him about was Oak, her best friend.

Some things were too precious. Oak was her secret.

Dad just blinked at her when she finished talking. His eyebrows sloped down and she could tell he didn't believe her.

"You don't believe me, do you?" she said sadly, staring at her shoes.

"Wait one second…" he said. He squeezed her shoulders and went over to where Dr. Vidal and the policewoman were talking.

When he came back, he gave her a hug.

"Dr. Vidal says you're telling the truth," Dad said. "I don't believe in fire spirits. But both of you say they exist. I can't think of another explanation."

Clarissa knew it would be hard for Dad to understand. So, she wrapped her arms around him and pressed her face into his green shirt. Then she sneezed.

"Bone dust?" he said, messing up her hair with his hand.

Did Dad just joke? Clarissa stared at him wide-eyed.

"I am so sorry I wouldn't listen to you," he said. "From now on, you can tell me anything. I promise to listen."

He kissed the top of her head.

It was like her old dad was back.

Chapter Eighteen

The police said Dad could take her home. He could put her bike in his car, so they walked to it. It was near the willow, which stood tall, but had black on its trunk.

"Dad, is the willow tree going to die?" she asked and looked at it sadly.

"It might be OK," he said.

"I don't want anyone to die," she said. "That's why I had to stop the ceremony. The fire spirit was going to burn up Dr. Vidal and Kurt."

"You are my brave girl," he said.

"Mum used to say that," Clarissa said.

"Yes, she did," he said. "Because it was true. And it still is."

Clarissa felt a smile curl on her lips. She liked this new Dad. She hoped he would stay.

He even agreed with the doctor about having ice cream for her throat.

When they got home Dad sent Mrs. Beech away after he told her Clarissa had a very good reason for going out when she did. Clarissa hid behind her Dad as Mrs. Beech tried to meet her eye. She felt bad about sneaking out on Mrs. Beech.

Edmund was already in bed, so it was just Dad and her eating ice cream in front of a normal fire.

"I can't believe Dr. Vidal would steal a potion from the museum," Dad said.

"It was really Kurt who stole it," Clarissa said. "He got away. I don't think that's fair."

"Dr. Vidal told the policewoman all about Kurt," Dad said. "They will both have to pay a big fine."

"So…they won't go to jail?" Clarissa said. She didn't like thinking of Dr. Vidal in jail, wearing overalls. She always wore nice clothes like flowery skirts and blouses.

"They probably won't go to jail," Dad said. "But Dr. Vidal will lose her job. Guess I will need to find a new assistant."

"Maybe I could be your assistant," Clarissa said. Then she could explore the basement collection anytime she wanted.

Dad smiled.

"When you're older, I would love that," he said and kissed her forehead.

She finished the ice cream, and curled up on the cushions with Shadow.

"I'm so tired all of a sudden," she said.

"You're a hero," he said, petting her hair. "Sleep. And I'm sorry again."

"For what?" she mumbled.

"Sorry I didn't listen to you," he said. "You should be able to tell me anything."

Clarissa smiled.

She slept deeply on the floor by the fire…

…until the fire spirit woke her up.

She heard it calling her, "Girl."

She sat up and rubbed her eyes. It was very dark except for the fireplace. A healthy orange fire crackled, and the face in the flames peered at her with shadow eyes.

"Hello," Clarissa said, with a tired smile. She was glad to see it, even though she was having a very deep, very comfortable sleep.

Shadow hissed at the fire from her side.

"It's OK, boy," she said, stroking his black, silky fur.

"When I first met you I thought you were a powerful girl to wake a fire spirit," Fire said. "I see now you are also very brave. You could have been burned, could have been killed. But you blazed bright and spoke your truth."

"I think speaking my truth worked. No one got hurt," Clarissa said. "And I think Dad's back."

"Was he gone?" Fire asked.

Clarissa sighed.

"When Mum died he changed," she said. "I lost Mum, but in a way, I lost Dad, too."

"I am sorry, little flame," Fire said, turning orange.

"I miss them both so much sometimes, it's a pain inside my heart," she said. She put a hand to her chest. "But maybe now Dad's back."

"I feel sadness too," Fire said. "I loved my parent. I was a little flame when my parent died," it said. "We were in a forest fire, burning all those pine trees. It was wonderful."

Clarissa shivered. She didn't like the thought of a burning forest.

"I was too greedy," Fire said. "I was near the top of the tree, burning, burning. But suddenly there was only a little bit left to burn."

"Why didn't you take your heart flame somewhere safe?" she asked.

"I was too weak," Fire said. "I would have gone out completely if my parent hadn't given me another tree. But my parent was also too weak to take its heart flame to safety."

"So, your parent died to save you?" she asked.

"Yes. My parent was old and weak," Fire said. "One thousand years my parent had flamed in the world. Many times my parent said it was ready to become a star."

Clarissa scooted closer to the warmth of the flames. Shadow came closer with her.

"My mum was weak when she was pregnant with Edmund," she said. "But she wanted to have the baby. The doctors warned her, but she did it anyway."

"Your parent died to save your brother?" Fire asked.

Clarissa nodded.

"So, your bravery comes from your mother," Fire said. "And I, much older and much bigger than you, have not been brave."

"You could be brave if you wanted," she said. "I just know it."

"If you believe I am brave then I must be brave," Fire said, shooting yellow sparks up the chimney. "I will grant the oak tree's wish."

"You'll bring back the will-o'-the-wisps?" Clarissa asked, excited.

"I feel I must," Fire said. "Or I will not be as brave as little flame."

Clarissa laughed. She added a log to the fire.

She curled up near the flames with Shadow while the fire spirit hummed. In the morning, she'd tell Oak the good news.

Three good things had happened today.

One, the potion bottle was found. Two, Dad had actually listened to her and made a joke. Three, now she had good news for the tree because the wisps would come back.

But one sad thing might have happened too.

If the fire spirit granted both their wishes, would it ever visit her again? Or would it leave her forever?

Chapter Nineteen

Clarissa slept on the cushions in the living room all night, until 10 am Monday morning. She was tired from all the smoke she breathed in. Dad let her stay home from school, and he stayed home from work. Edmund got to stay home too, though, of course he didn't know why.

Clarissa ate some cereal. She went out to the garden just before noon.

Oak yawned and groaned as soon as Clarissa said hello. She launched into the story of saving the potion bottle from the fire spirit.

"You are a brave girl," the tree said, patting her

shoulder with its leaves. "But you could have gotten hurt."

"I am fine," Clarissa said. "I just have a scratchy throat. Dad says I can have ice cream after lunch."

"And your dad, he believes in the fire spirit now?" the tree asked.

"He says he doesn't know what to believe," Clarissa said.

The tree yawned, making a sound like a bear roaring. It stretched its branches and its leaves shook.

"Why are you so tired?" Clarissa asked.

"My talking time is almost done," Oak said.

"Oh," Clarissa said. "I will come back later." She started to tiptoe away, so the tree could get some rest.

"No, little sapling," Oak said. "Soon I will speak no more."

"You mean you will not speak ever again?" Her voice came out high and whispery. Her throat tightened. Tears filled her eyes.

"But you're my best friend!" she said.

"Three years is a long time for a tree to talk," Oak said. "Soon I will be a normal tree, asleep inside."

Clarissa stared at her muddy shoes.

"Well, this is a sad day now," she said. "It was going to be a happy day, especially because you got your wish."

"The fire spirit will return will-o'-the-wisps to the land?" Oak said. "Then it is a very happy day. Many humans and animals who are lost in the dark will find their way, guided by a wisp." The tree stretched its branches high.

Clarissa sniffed.

"But you're going to stop talking to me," she said.

The tree opened its branches to her.

"You have lost much for one so young," it said. "But I will still be here, watching and loving you. And if you need me to, I will start to talk again."

"I need you to talk to me now!" Clarissa said, and stamped her foot.

"No, sapling," the tree said. "You do not need me anymore."

Clarissa didn't want to hug the tree, even though its branches were wide open for a hug. She was angry.

So, she went into the house. She heard the tree give a deep woody sigh.

"Was that the wind?" her dad said from his armchair. "I thought there wasn't much wind today."

"It was the oak tree," Clarissa said, trying the truth. She plopped on her cushions on the floor. Dad just blinked at her.

The fire in the fireplace made the living room warm and cozy. But the flames didn't have a face.

Who was she going to talk to, with the tree asleep and the fire spirit gone?

Chapter Twenty

Clarissa didn't know what she wanted to do. She didn't want to read or write to Mum.

She just wanted to be sad.

Her shoulders slumped, and she buried her face in the cushions. Tears ran into the cushion covers. She would miss talking to Oak so much.

She felt the pressure of a hand on her back. When she looked up, Dad was next to her.

"Are you still tired from yesterday?" he asked.

Clarissa nodded. She watched, amazed, as Dad did something she hadn't seen him do in years.

He sat on the floor. But he found it hard to do.

He kept shifting his feet and legs around. Finally he got two cushions under him and could sit still.

Edmund gazed at them from the sofa. His mouth was open, like he was amazed too.

"Honey, I wondered if you could make those fantastic pancakes for lunch," Dad said.

"Yeah, I think I could," she said, trying to remember the recipe.

"Well, that would be wonderful," he said. "After that we'll all go out for ice cream."

"Don't you…don't you have to work?" she asked. They almost never went out without going to his museum office too.

"What I have to do is spoil my hero daughter a little," he said. He kissed her forehead.

Clarissa felt stunned when she went into the kitchen. Dad was being so nice, which made her happy. But Oak was going to stop talking to her, which made her sad. So, she was both happy and sad, and it was confusing.

She turned on the stove and started cooking. When her name was called through the flames, she jumped.

"Girl," the high voice of the fire spirit through the stovetop called.

"You're back!" Clarissa said, feeling a happy warmth in her heart.

"I went to the Earth's core again," Fire said. "I bathed in molten lava."

"That doesn't sound like something I would like, but I'm happy for you," Clarissa said. She had three pancakes done already. They were rounder than the first time she made them.

Clarissa took a deep breath. She decided to be honest.

"I was afraid you might never come back," she said. "After all, you granted my wish and Oak's wish."

The flame in the burner turned orange.

"Little flame," Fire said in a high, stretched voice. "You have taught me to be brave. Now I believe you could teach me to be a friend."

"So...you'll keep visiting me?" Clarissa said, her heart skipping. She could hardly believe it, it was such happy news.

"I would like to visit my human friend Clarissa," Fire said. "As long as I can roam the Earth too."

"I would like that too," Clarissa said. "Maybe you can teach me to make something more than pancakes?"

The fire in the burner turned bright yellow and sparked. Clarissa had to put out a little flame on her apron.

"I would like that," Fire said in its squeaky voice. "Yes, I can teach you more tasty food to make. We can use the hearth fire, not these tiny flames."

Clarissa felt happiness flood her heart. Not only would she learn to make tasty meals, her friend the fire spirit would hang around and help her out.

She felt so happy that she decided to forgive Oak. After all, it wasn't its fault. It was getting tired and it was true that trees don't normally talk. It wasn't fair to blame it for being a tree.

After the pancakes, which even Shadow tasted, Clarissa went outside. The tree was waiting for her.

It opened its branches to her.

She gave it a big tree-hug.

"I love you," she said into Oak's trunk.

She thought it was done talking. But it surprised her.

"I love you, too" Oak said in a very quiet voice. The leaves rustled and a red one fell into her palm.

Oak breathed in deep. She felt the trunk tremble. Then it was still.

A tear slid down Clarissa's cheek as she looked at her friend's leaves. They were turning yellow and red, and would soon fall.

Long branches lifted from across the garden. It was the willow tree. It looked like it was inviting her to come to it.

She carefully walked to the tree, remembering how it was afraid of humans. The long branches curled around her, and gathered her to its trunk for a hug. Clarissa hugged the willow back.

When she looked up, she swore an eye in the bark winked at her.

She walked back to the house. She waved at Willow, who waved a branch back.

Her tears dried as she sat on the cushions and pet Shadow. She had lost one tree friend but gained another. The fire spirit was going to teach her to cook. Dad was paying attention to her again.

So, life was pretty good, all in all.

"OK, darlings, who wants to go for ice cream?" Dad said, walking into the living room smiling. He knelt down next to Clarissa.

"Me!" Edmund said, and climbed down from the sofa.

"Did you just…speak?" Dad asked, and Edmund came over to them.

Shadow stared at him as he climbed into Clarissa's lap.

"Me!" Edmund said louder. "I want I cream!"

Clarissa and her dad met each other's eyes. Then they both laughed, and hugged Edmund. He giggled as they tickled him.

"What a day!" Clarissa said out loud.

Shadow meowed happily and climbed from Clarissa's knee to Edmund's lap and licked Dad's hand. He could visit all three of them at once, because they sat so close to each other.

For once, the whole family was together.

Well, almost the whole family. Clarissa jumped up and ran to her bedroom. She took the special journal with the jasmine flowers on it out of the drawer of her night table.

She went downstairs and sat next to Dad, Edmund and Shadow. And she plopped the journal in front of Dad.

"I write Mum in this," she said. "I wanted you to see. Now she's here with us too."

Dad looked at her with his eyebrows raised.

"One minute…" he said, and he got up and left the room.

He came back with a big, black binder. Inside were typed, printed letters.

"I email her, and print them out," he said.

Clarissa couldn't believe it. All this time, they were both writing Mum.

"Should I read you a story before we go for ice cream?" he asked. "We used to do that."

Clarissa felt too old to be read to. Edmund would like it, though. But another idea brightened in her mind.

"I tell Edmund about Mum sometimes," Clarissa said. "Maybe you can tell a story about her."

"How about…the story of how we met?" Dad asked.

Clarissa's heart skipped happily.

"I love that story," Clarissa said. "I think I still remember it from when you and Mum told it."

"Well, you can help me tell your brother," Dad said. "I was in class one day at university and I saw this beautiful woman with long, light-brown hair in front of me..."

Clarissa clapped.

Not only was Dad back, the stories were back. The stories about Mum.

A week later, the night was clear, so Dad took Clarissa and Edmund out to star gaze. He pointed out the constellations to them. Clarissa showed Edmund the North Star. Dad was impressed she remembered it.

As usual, she gave Oak a hug. Even though Oak didn't speak anymore, she knew Oak could feel it.

She waved to Willow, who curtsied, her branches fanned out elegantly.

Dad was trying to find the Seven Sisters constellations when Edmund bounced up and down.

135

"Star!" Edmund said. He was pointing to a bright object that looked like a star. The only difference was, it was near to the ground and moving around him.

"Edmund, that could be a will-o'-the-wisp!" she said.

The light moved away, and Edmund followed.

"Dad, let's follow the wisp," Clarissa said.

"My goodness, what is that?" Dad said when he saw it. "I've never seen anything like it."

"Just come with us," Clarissa said.

The wisp was getting faster. It sped ahead and then waited for Edmund to catch up. Then it sped up again.

"Looks like it's going towards the river," Dad said, scooping Edmund up. Now they could follow more quickly.

As they neared the river, they entered fog. Dad took Clarissa's hand. Sometimes people got lost in river fog.

All she could see was thick dark fog, but Edmund kept urging them forwards. Every now and then she'd catch sight of a bright star in front of them.

"We should be careful," Dad said. "People walk right into the river in this type of fog."

"The wisp will lead us safely," Clarissa said. She hoped it was true. She knew sometimes wisps played tricks on people.

A high whine reached her ears. Dad picked up speed.

"Someone's crying," he said as Clarissa ran alongside.

They came to a little boy slightly older than Edmund, standing alone by the water. He stopped crying when he saw them.

The star-like wisp danced in front of him, and he smiled big through his tears. He tried to catch it, but it danced away.

"No catch!" Edmund said strongly, from Dad's arms.

Clarissa took a close look at the boy.

"That's Preeti's brother," she said. "Jay, right? I remember you from the ice cream shop."

The boy nodded. He started to sniffle again.

"Want to go home," he said.

Dad found Preeti's mum's number on a parents' group he had never used before. It took him a while, but he found it.

Clarissa could hear Preeti's mum making happy noises over the phone as Dad told her they found Jay.

Preeti's house was close by. Clarissa took Jay's hand and they walked there together.

As soon as the front door opened, Preeti's mum rushed out and gave him a giant hug. Preeti hugged Clarissa, and thanked her with big eyes.

"We were so worried," Preeti said. "He was gone for an hour and we looked everywhere."

Clarissa, Edmund and Dad were invited in. The house smelled like spices. Preeti's mum said she was cooking with cinnamon, cardamom and lemongrass.

"Do you like to cook?" Preeti's mum asked her.

"I do," Clarissa said. "I can only make pancakes, though."

"Well, I can help with that," Preeti's mum said and winked. "I will teach you to make onion bhajis, an Indian snack. Come on!"

That night they ate well. The food was tasty and there were lots of vegetables.

Clarissa sat next to Preeti and told her about her adventures. Preeti kept saying "wow" as Clarissa told her about the museum basement.

"That's just the beginning!" Clarissa said.

Clarissa told her about the stolen potion and the fire ceremony. When she got to the part about the fire spirit burning the fire bright, Preeti play-punched her arm.

"A fire spirit!" Preeti said, laughing. "I love your stories."

Preeti didn't believe her. But it didn't matter.

Clarissa had fun hearing Preeti's "wows".

"I have a secret," Clarissa said, making her voice as small as the fire spirit when it spoke through the kitchen stovetop.

"What?" Preeti asked, leaning in.

"I'm going to speak up in class now," Clarissa said. "I'm going to fan my flame."

Preeti hugged her.

"That's what I've been telling you to do all along!" Preeti said.

When it was time to go, Preeti's mum gave Clarissa the onion bhaji recipe.

She invited them for weekly dinner.

Clarissa's heart sang when Dad said yes.

They would eat a good dinner every week. Preeti said they could play a game next time. Things were getting better and better.

Dad picked up Edmund for the walk home.

Clarissa skipped as she held Dad's hand. The fog cleared once they left the river. But she kept holding on to him.

And he kept holding on to her.

Thank you

Thank you for helping with early drafts of Clarissa: John Spudich, Katrina Dring, Kim Ellis, St. Albans School, Cambridge—Jessica Brett and the year 3 class Autumn 2020 and Bluestem Montessori School, Lincoln, Nebraska.

Thank you for purchasing and reading *Clarissa*.

Handersen Publishing is an independent publishing house that specializes in creating quality young adult, middle grade, and picture books.

We hope you enjoyed this book and will consider leaving a review on Amazon or Goodreads. A small review can make a big difference.

Thank you.

About the Author

Giulietta M. Spudich lives in Cambridge, England where she moved from California, US in 2002. She loves writing stories that connect with nature and the elements. Zeta, a Catalan Sheepdog retired from herding goats in the mountains, kindly agreed to pose for this photo.

Find Giulietta on Twitter @spudichpen and Facebook @GiuliettaBooks.

Discover more at:
www.ElementGirls.org

Imaginative and engaging magical fiction.
-Kirkus Review

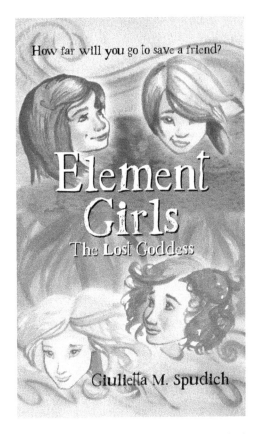

How far will **you** go to save a friend?

Element Girls
The Lost Goddess

Giulietta M. Spudich

"A great story that empowers girls and shows that their friendship and love for each other can help them overcome obstacles."

-Lisa-Anne L. Tsuruda–
'Iolani School, Honolulu, Hawaii

Also by Giulietta M. Spudich
The Giant Series

Friendship can come in the most unlikely of places.

The Amber GIANT

Story Monsters Approved!
SM
StoryMonsters.com

Giulietta M. Spudich

A unique story to take your children out of their everyday world.

"The Amber Giant is an inspirational story for children and pre-teens that combines adventure, learning, and lessons in kindness and friendship. It's a captivating, highly creative read that will mesmerize your children with a unique plotline that will take them out of their everyday world. A fun story for adults too! I highly recommend."

-5 stars, Amazon Customer Review

A whimsical adventure that promotes individuality and self-acceptance.

-Kirkus Review

Elika is meant to be so much more than normal.

The Ice Giant

Giulietta M. Spudich

"Lovely inter-generation story starring moody, 13-year old Elika. She's finding her place in the world, in her family and finding out what's important to her. Great to read a book featuring strong female characters who form a supportive and interesting family lineage (daughter, mother, aunt and features memories of grandma)."

-5 stars, Goodreads Review

Handersen Publishing

Great books for young readers!

www.handersenpublishing.com

Lightning Source UK Ltd.
Milton Keynes UK
UKHW011005301020
372510UK00001B/53